This
Treasure Cove Story
belongs to

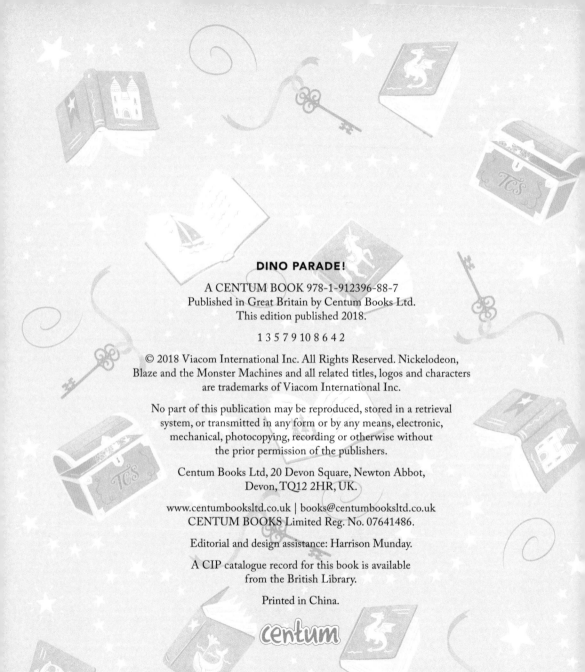

DINO PARADE!

A CENTUM BOOK 978-1-912396-88-7
Published in Great Britain by Centum Books Ltd.
This edition published 2018.

1 3 5 7 9 10 8 6 4 2

© 2018 Viacom International Inc. All Rights Reserved. Nickelodeon,
Blaze and the Monster Machines and all related titles, logos and characters
are trademarks of Viacom International Inc.

No part of this publication may be reproduced, stored in a retrieval
system, or transmitted in any form or by any means, electronic,
mechanical, photocopying, recording or otherwise without
the prior permission of the publishers.

Centum Books Ltd, 20 Devon Square, Newton Abbot,
Devon, TQ12 2HR, UK.

www.centumbooksltd.co.uk | books@centumbooksltd.co.uk
CENTUM BOOKS Limited Reg. No. 07641486.

Editorial and design assistance: Harrison Munday.

A CIP catalogue record for this book is available
from the British Library.

Printed in China.

centum

nickelodeon

A Treasure Cove Story

DINO PARADE!

Adapted by Mary Tillworth

Based on the teleplay 'Dinosaur Parade' by Gabe Pulliam

Illustrated by Heather Martinez

One sunny morning in Axle City, Blaze and
AJ hurried to the parade grounds. Their friend
Zeg was leading an earth-shaking, wheel-stomping
dinosaur parade!

Sneaky Crusher wanted to be in the parade, too.
He put on a dinosaur costume and crept in front
of the T rex.

'Here comes the Crusher-saurus!' he shouted.

Just then, the dinosaur costume slipped down over Crusher's eyes and he crashed into a stack of barrels. Oil poured out onto the street.

'Gaskets! That oil is making the dinosaurs slide out of control!' warned Blaze.

The dinosaurs slid into a bunch of balloons that had come loose and started to float away!

'Help!' cried the dinosaurs as they floated away, too.
'Blaze! AJ!' cried Zeg. 'Zeg friends in trouble!'
Blaze zoomed over to his buddy. 'Don't worry, Zeg!
AJ and I can help you rescue your dinosaur friends.'

Blaze, AJ and Zeg raced after the dinosaurs.
'Look!' shouted AJ. Two ankylosauruses and
one stegosaurus were soaring towards a crane
at a construction site.
'Zeg coming, dinosaurs!' yelled Zeg.

Blaze noticed a pile of barrels next to a seesaw with a box on one end.

'I know how we can rescue the dinosaurs – with a chain reaction! A chain reaction is when the energy from one action makes something else happen,' he said.

Blaze and AJ started a chain reaction by pushing over the barrels.

The barrels fell onto the seesaw. The seesaw tossed the box up and the box hit the crane. The crane swung and grabbed an ankylosaurus out of the air!

Using the chain reaction, Blaze and AJ saved all
three dinosaurs.
'You go back to parade now,' Zeg told the dinos.
'Blaze and AJ help Zeg find other dinosaur friends.'

Blaze and Zeg drove off
to search for the rest of the
dinosaurs. They saw two
stegosauruses and one
ankylosaurus drifting into
a long tunnel.

'Quick!' said AJ. 'We need
to follow them.' The Monster
Machines hopped onto
a motor boat and sped
after them.

Inside the tunnel, it got colder and colder.
'Brrrr,' said Zeg.
There was ice everywhere! On the walls,
on the ceiling – and even in the water!
Ice chunks smashed into the boat again and again.

'If we're not careful, the ice will sink our boat,'
said Blaze. 'We've got to find a way to blast this ice.'

'I know!' AJ sketched out a blueprint with his skywriter gloves. 'We can use a water cannon to break up the ice!'

Blaze quickly transformed himself. 'I'm a water-cannon Monster Machine!' With a few powerful pumps, Blaze blasted the ice to pieces!

At the end of the tunnel, Blaze slowed down.
He stopped under the three floating dinosaurs.

'Hang on dinosaurs! Zeg get you down!' shouted
Zeg. He revved his engine. With a burst of speed, he
zoomed up the tunnel wall.

Zeg bashed through the balloons. *Pop! Pop! Pop!*
All three dinosaurs landed safely next to Blaze.
'Woo-hoo!' they cheered as Zeg zoomed back
to the boat.

'Now c'mon, dinosaurs,' said Blaze. 'Let's get to the parade!'

Zeg, Blaze and AJ needed to find the last missing dinosaur – a T rex named Fluffy. Back at the parade, AJ switched on his Visor View.

'Uh-oh,' said Zeg. 'Fluffy's balloons go *pop*!'

'Hubcaps!' gasped Blaze. 'Fluffy is stuck at the top of Axle City Tower! We need to use Blazing Speed to get to the tower super fast. Let's *blaaaze*!'

The Monster Machines zoomed to the tower.
'This way, guys!' Blaze drove to a lift. 'If we push the
green button, the lift will take us up to the next level.'
Zeg pressed the green button and they got in.
'Going up!'

The lift rocketed skyward. But the Monster Machines were only halfway to the top of the tower. And the button they needed to push to continue to the top was on the ceiling!

'How are we going to press it?' asked AJ.

'To press the button, we'll need one more chain reaction,' said Blaze.

Outside the lift, Blaze saw some items they could use for the chain reaction. Blaze bumped a cart against a ladder and the ladder wobbled. A bowling ball on top of the ladder fell onto a trampoline and the ball bounced up and hit the green button on the lift ceiling!

Blaze and Zeg jumped into the lift and the doors closed.
'Whoa-ho-ho!' laughed the Monster Machines as the lift shot up again.
'We made it to the top of the tower!' said Blaze.

When the lift doors opened, Blaze and Zeg were at the top of Axle City Tower.

'Help!' cried Fluffy. He was trapped!
'Don't worry, Fluffy. We get you down!' said Zeg.
Blaze and Zeg tossed their tow hooks over the pointy top of the tower. Together the Monster Machines pulled with all their might.

They slowly bent the top of the tower
down… down… down and Fluffy hopped
to safety!
    'Now we just need a way to get Fluffy
to the parade,' said Blaze.
    Zeg grinned. 'Oooh! Zeg have idea!'

Back at the parade grounds, the crowd saw three shapes in the sky. Blaze, Zeg and Fluffy were floating down with parachutes!

'They made it!' cheered the crowd.

Zeg laughed. 'Zeg so happy dinosaurs back together again!'
'Hey, dinosaurs!' called Blaze. 'Now that you're all here,
what do you say we finish the dinosaur parade?'

Zeg whipped out his baton and began to twirl it.
'Follow Zeg!' he said proudly.

The dinosaurs roared and stomped and shook their tails.
Thanks to Blaze, AJ and Zeg, it was the best dino parade ever!

Treasure Cove Stories

•*Book list may be subject to change.*